BONY-LEGS

Joanna Cole

PICTURES BY

Dirk Zimmer

SCHOLASTIC INC.
New York Toronto London Auckland Sydney

In the folktales of Russia a witch called Baba Yaga,
nicknamed the Bony-Legged One, often appears.
The story in this book is based on the tale "Baba-Yaga"
in *Russian Fairy Tales* by Aleksandr Afanas'ev.

ISBN 0-590-40516-0

Text Copyright ©1983 by Joanna Cole.
Illustrations ©1983 by Dirk Zimmer.

12 11   1 2 3 4 5/9

Printed in the U.S.A.   23

TO RACHEL
J. C.

TO DIANA
D. Z.

Bony-Legs was
a horrible, bad witch.
She could run very fast
on her bony old legs.
Her teeth were
made of iron,
and she liked to
eat little children.
She lived
deep in the woods
in a hut
that stood on
chicken feet.

All day long
she waited
for children
to pass by.

On the edge
of the same woods
a girl named Sasha
lived with her aunt.
One morning Sasha's aunt
sent her out
to borrow
a needle and thread.

Sasha took
some bread and butter
and a bit of meat
for lunch.
She began to walk.

She walked and walked.
She was surprised
when she came
to a hut that stood
on chicken feet.

She decided
to go inside.
She opened the gate.
It creaked and groaned.
"Poor gate," said Sasha.
"You need some grease."
She scraped the butter
from her bread
and rubbed it
on the hinges
of the gate.
It opened quietly.

Sasha walked
up the path.
A skinny dog
stood in her way.
It barked and barked.
"Poor dog," said Sasha.
"You look hungry."
She gave her bread
to the dog.
He ate it up
and did not bark again.

A cat was sitting
near the hut
mewing sadly.
"Poor kitty," said Sasha.
"Are you hungry too?"
She gave her meat
to the cat.
Old Bony-Legs
poked her head
out the window.
"What do you want?"
she asked Sasha.

"My aunt
would like to borrow
a needle and thread,"
said Sasha.
"Come right in,"
said the witch.
Sasha went inside.

"Now," said Bony-Legs,
"get into the tub."
"Why?" asked Sasha.
"I don't need a bath."
"I want you
   nice and clean,"
   said Bony-Legs.
"I'm going to cook you
   for my supper."
She grinned and showed
her iron teeth.
Then she went outside
to gather sticks
for the fire.
She locked the door
behind her.

Sasha was scared.

She began to cry.

"Don't cry,"

said a voice.

"I will help you."

Sasha looked around.

No one was there

but the cat.

"Fill the tub

but don't get in,"

said the cat.

Sasha had never heard

a cat talk,

but she did

what it told her.

Bony-Legs called
through the door,
"Are you washing, girl?"

"Yes, I am,"
said Sasha.
"Good," said Bony-Legs.
And she went away
to gather more sticks.

After she had gone
the cat gave Sasha
a silver mirror.
"When you are in trouble,
throw this away,"
said the cat.

That does not make sense,
thought Sasha.
But she took
the mirror
and put it
in her pocket.
"Now run,"
said the cat.
Sasha climbed
out the window
and began to run.

The witch called
through the door again,
"Are you washing, girl?"

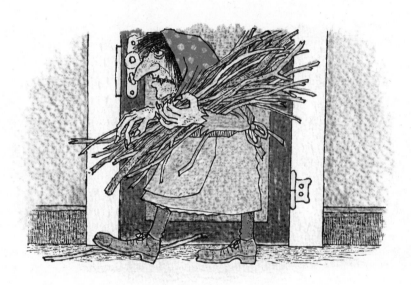

"Yes, I am,"
said the cat.
"Well, hurry up,"
said Bony-Legs.
Then she went away.

Sasha ran through
the yard.
The dog stopped her
and gave her
a wooden comb.
"When you need help,
throw this away,"
said the dog.

That does not make sense,
thought Sasha.
But she put the comb
in her pocket.
Then she opened
the gate.
It did not make
a sound
on its buttered hinges.
Sasha ran
into the woods.

Bony-Legs called
through the door again,
"Are you washing, girl?"

"Yes, I am,"
  said the cat.
"What!" said Bony-Legs.
"Not done yet?"
  She flung open the door.

There was the cat.

There was the tub.

But where was Sasha?

"You sneaky cat!"

yelled Bony-Legs.

"Why did you trick me?"

"You never fed me,"
said the cat.
"But Sasha gave me
meat to eat."
"Bah!" said Bony-Legs,
and she ran into the yard.
The dog was sleeping
in the sun.
"You lazy dog!"
shouted Bony-Legs.
"Why didn't you bark
at her?"
"You never fed me,"
said the dog.

"But Sasha gave me

bread to eat."

"Bah!" said the witch,

and she rushed to the gate.

"You worthless gate!"

she screamed.

"Why didn't you
   lock her in?"
"You never took care
   of me,"
   said the gate.
"But Sasha put butter
   on my hinges."

The old witch
flew into a rage.
She stamped her feet,
pulled her hair,
and even pinched
her own nose.
But she did not feel
any better.

She ran after Sasha
on her bony old legs.
Sasha looked back
and saw the witch's
iron teeth
glinting in the sun.

Sasha was scared.
She remembered
the silver mirror.
She took it
out of her pocket
and threw it
behind her.

The mirror became
a deep silver lake.
Bony-Legs could not
cross it.

She ran home
and got her tub.

She rowed it
across the lake

and ran after Sasha
on her bony old legs.

Sasha saw the witch
coming again.
She remembered
the wooden comb.

She took it
out of her pocket
and threw it
behind her.

The comb grew
until it was as tall
as three trees.
Bony-Legs
could not climb
over it.

She could not dig

under it.

She could not even

squeeze through it.

At last
she gave up.
And she stamped her feet,
pulled her hair,
and pinched her nose
all the way back
to her hut.

Sasha went home, too.
And you can be sure
she never went back
to the hut that stood
on chicken feet.

And for as long
as she lived
she never saw
old Bony-Legs
again.